Stories for 5 Year Olds

This is a Parragon Publishing Book
First published in 2000

Parragon Publishing
Queen Street House, 4 Queen Street,
Bath, BA1 1HE, UK

Produced by The Templar Company plc
Pippbrook Mill, London Road, Dorking,
Surrey, RH4 1JE, UK

Printed and bound in Spain
ISBN 0 75254 070 X

Stories for 5 Year Olds

p

Contents

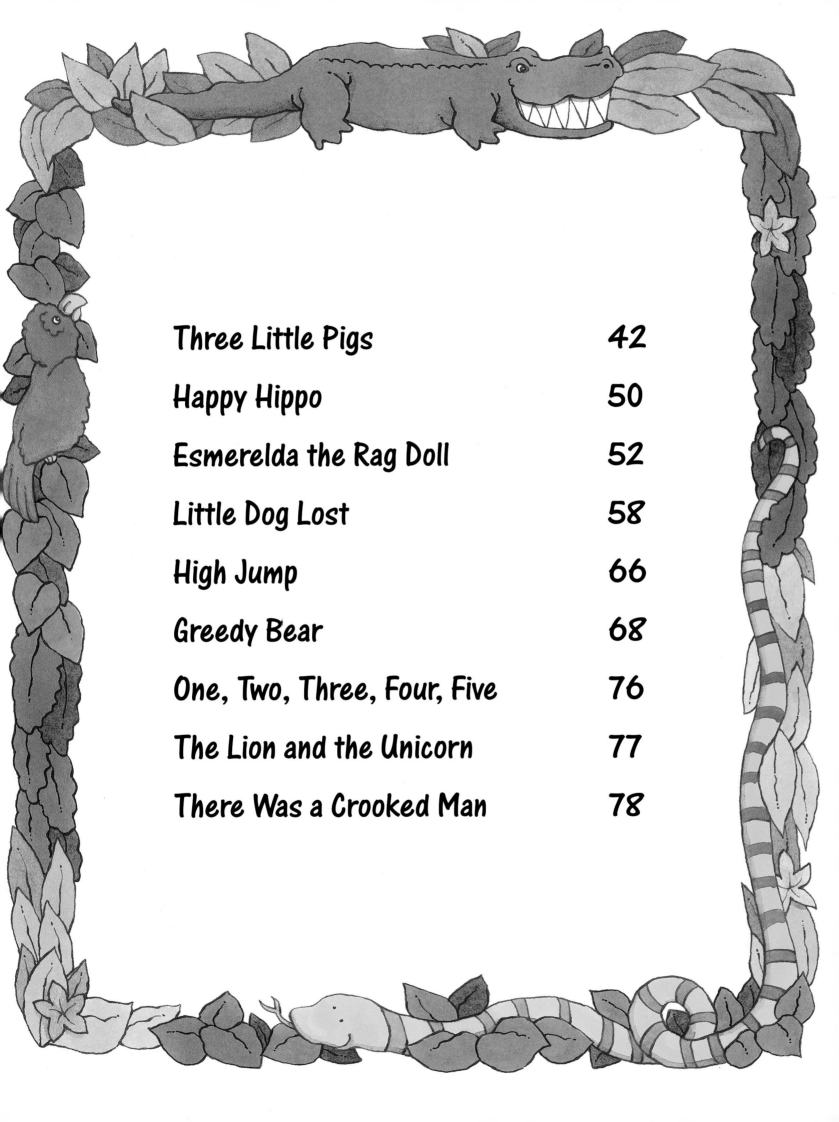

Sing a Song of Sixpence

Sing a song of sixpence,

A pocket full of rye;

Four-and-twenty blackbirds baked in a pie;

When the pie was opened,

The birds began to sing;

Wasn't that a dainty dish,

To set before a king?

Old King Cole

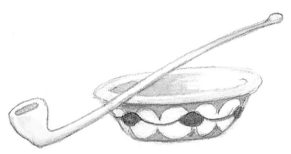

Old King Cole was a merry old soul,

And a merry old soul was he;

He called for his pipe,

And he called for his bowl,

And he called for his fiddlers three.

Bobby Shaftoe

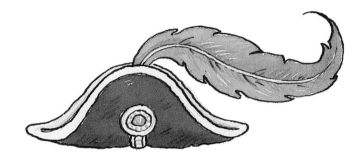

Bobby Shaftoe's gone to sea,
Silver buckles at his knee,
He'll come back and marry me,
Bonny Bobby Shaftoe.

Little Jack Horner

Little Jack Horner,

Sat in a corner,

Eating a Christmas pie.

He put in his thumb,

And pulled out a plum,

And said, "What a good boy am I!"

Morag the Witch

Morag was just an ordinary witch – until the day she enrolled for a course of advanced spell casting at the Wizard, Witch and Warlock Institute of Magic. For that was where she met Professor Fizzlestick. Now Professor Fizzlestick was a very wise old man indeed. Morag, on the other hand, was a very vain young witch who didn't know as much as she thought she did. She could turn people into frogs if they really deserved it, and do other simple spells like that, but she still had a lot to learn. The problem was, Morag thought she was the most perfect little witch in the whole wide world.

Morag's adventure started on her very first day at school. At the beginning of the day, after all the young witches and wizards had made friends and met the teachers, they were called in one by one to talk to Professor Fizzlestick.

"Now, young Morag Bendlebaum, I taught both your mother and your father," said the professor in a very serious voice, "and a very fine witch and wizard they turned out to be, too. So, what kind of witch do you think you are going to be?"

Without giving this any thought at all, Morag blurted out, "I'm better than my parents, and I'm probably better than you!"

This answer surprised even Morag, for although she thought this was true, she didn't actually mean to say it.

"Don't be surprised by your answers," said Professor Fizzlestick, "there is a truth spell in this room, and whatever you truly believe you must say. And I have to say that you appear to have an enormously high opinion of yourself. Why don't you tell me what makes you so very good?"

"I'm clever," said Morag, "and I'm good, and I'm always right."

"But what about your dark side?" said Professor Fizzlestick.

"I'm sorry to disappoint you," replied Morag quite seriously, "but I'm afraid I simply don't have a dark side."

11

"Well in that case I would like you to meet someone very close to you," said Professor Fizzlestick with a smile on his lips.

Morag looked over to where Professor Fizzlestick pointed, and was startled to see on the sofa next to her… herself!

As Morag stared open-mouthed with astonishment, the professor explained that if, as she believed, she was without a dark side, then there was absolutely nothing to worry about. "If, however," he continued, "you have deceived yourself, then I'm afraid you are in for a few surprises."

With that the professor dismissed them both from the room and told them to get to know each other. As Morag and her dark side stood outside the professor's room, Morag's dark side jumped and whooped for joy. "At last," she cried, "I'm free. I don't have to sit and listen to you telling me what's right all day; I don't have to keep persuading you to choose the biggest slice of cake before your brother – in fact, I don't, I repeat **don't,** have to do anything that you tell me at all."

So saying she broke into a run and rushed down the corridor, knocking over chairs and bumping into other little witches and wizards along the way. Morag was horrified. She would have to follow her dark side and stop her from causing trouble. Morag chased after her dark side and finally caught up with her at the chocolate machine. "Don't eat all that chocolate," cried Morag. "You know it's bad for your teeth and will ruin your appetite for lunch!"

"Tsk!" scoffed her dark side. "You might not want any chocolate but I certainly do!" And with that she ran off once more, dropping chocolate on to the freshly polished floor as well as pushing a big piece into her mouth.

Just then, the bell sounded for lunch. Although Morag felt she ought to find her dark side, she also knew that the bell was a command to go to the dining hall, and she mustn't disobey it. Morag sat down to lunch next to her friend, Topaz. She was just about to tell her what had happened, when she saw that Topaz was not eating her vegetables! Morag scolded Topaz for this, and gave her a lecture on eating healthily.

Topaz stared at Morag in amazement, then peered closely at her. "What's happened to you?" she asked.

Morag explained what had happened in Professor Fizzlestick's office, and then declared, "And you know, it's the best thing that has ever happened to me. I thought I was good before, but now I'm even better. I never want my dark side back again, but we must find her and lock her up so that she can do no harm."

Topaz agreed that they must find her dark side, but secretly hoped that she and Morag would be re-united. Morag wasn't Morag without her dark side.

After lunch, Morag went for her first lesson of the afternoon. When she walked into the classroom she discovered her dark side already there, busy preparing spells! Morag's dark side had already prepared a 'turning a nose into an elephant's trunk' spell and a 'turning skin into dragons' scales' spell and was just finishing off a 'turning your teacher into stone' spell!

Morag suddenly heard a trumpeting noise from the back of the classroom. She turned to find that the wizard twins, Denzil and Dorian Dillydally, had both sprouted huge gray trunks down to the ground where their noses had been. Morag rushed over to her dark side to make her change them back, but before she could reach her she tripped over a creature crouching down on the floor. It looked just like a dragon and it was wearing a purple and white spotted dress last seen on Betina Bumblebag. Morag's dark side was casting spells all over the place. "Oh, why doesn't the teacher stop her!" cried Morag to Topaz.

I'm sure you've guessed by now. Nice Miss Chuckle was entirely turned to stone from head to foot!

Just then Professor Fizzlestick walked into the classroom. Morag pointed to her dark side, still making spells at the front of the classroom.

14

"Lock her up immediately," Morag begged the professor.

"I'm afraid that you are the only one who can do that," said the wise old man. "The two of you are inseparable and you need each other. Without your dark side you would be unbearable and without you she is dreadful. Have I your permission to lock her back inside you?"

Even though Morag didn't want any part of her dark side back, she agreed reluctantly. Her dark side instantly disappeared, and Morag felt... wonderful! Oh, it was so good to be back to normal, to be basically good, but occasionally mischievous.

"Thank you," said Morag to the professor. "I think I've learned something very valuable today."

"There is good and bad in everyone," replied the professor, "even the most perfect of witches."

Morag blushed when she remembered what she had said earlier that morning, but she was so relieved to find she was normal that she really didn't mind. Morag and Topaz went back to the classroom to undo all the bad things Morag's dark side had done, but on the way they both felt a huge urge for a snack, so they stopped at the chocolate machine first!

Catswhiskers

Catswhiskers was a pajama case cat, and a very fine-looking pajama case cat at that. Susie's granny had sewn him together when Susie was only four years old. It had taken Susie's granny quite a long time to make Catswhiskers. Every night she had sat by the fire carefully cutting and sewing, until he was perfect. Catswhiskers' body was made from the finest black velvet. He had beautiful red glass eyes, a bushy tail and the longest whiskers you have ever seen. That is how he got the name Catswhiskers. Catswhiskers sat on the end of Susie's bed, looking at all the toys in the bedroom in that slightly snooty way that cats have of looking at things.

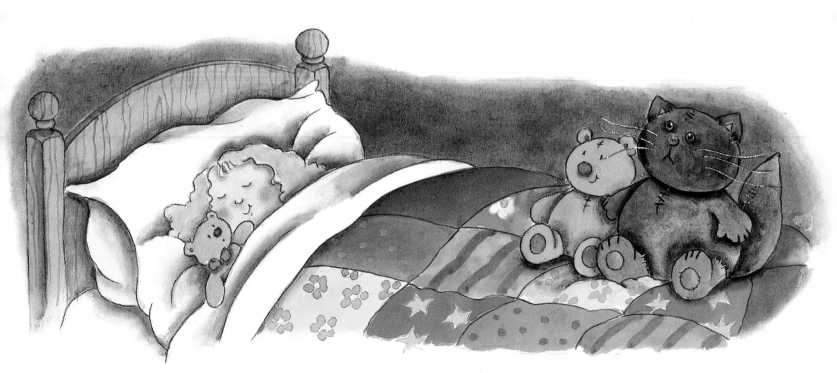

When Susie was asleep, or playing in another room, Catswhiskers and all the toys would talk to each other. But Catswhiskers was bored with talking to the toys. Jenny the rag doll was – well – just a rag doll. "What could a rag doll possibly have to say that would be of interest to a velvet pajama case cat?" thought Catswhiskers.

Then there was Neddy the rocking horse. He was a perfectly pleasant rocking horse as far as rocking horses went, but he only ever seemed to want to talk about how nice and shiny he was, and how he thought he was Susie's favorite toy. Even the alphabet bricks, the jack-in-the-box and the brightly colored ball seemed to have nothing to say of interest to Catswhiskers. He sighed and looked at the window, wondering if life was more exciting outside.

One day, he decided he'd had enough of life in the bedroom with all the toys, and that he would venture outside to see if he could meet someone more interesting to talk to. So that night, when it was dark and Susie was asleep, he crept carefully to the open bedroom window and jumped out. It was a clear, cold, moonlit night. Catswhiskers shivered a little to find it so cold outside, and he maybe shivered a little more because he was also rather frightened. But he was very excited to be in the outside world, too, and he soon forgot about the cold and his fear.

He walked along the fence to the end of Susie's garden and jumped down into the garden next door. He had no sooner landed when he heard a fierce growl and saw two big, black eyes glinting in the moonlight.

It was Barker, next door's dog – and he didn't like cats at all. With a loud bark, Barker came rushing towards Catswhiskers. His mouth was open wide and Catswhiskers could see his big, sharp teeth. In fact, he thought that he could see all the way down into Barker's stomach! Catswhiskers only just had time to leap back on to the fence as Barker, jaws still snapping, gave chase.

"Phew, what a narrow escape," gasped Catswhiskers. "I didn't realize dogs were so unfriendly!"

He was wondering where it might be safe to go next when he heard a low, hissing voice behind him. "Hey, velvet cat," hissed the voice. "What do you think you are doing on *our* patch?"

Catswhiskers turned around to see the biggest, meanest-looking cat he had ever set eyes on. And behind *him* were several more mean-looking cats, all coming slowly towards Catswhiskers with their sharp claws at the ready. Catswhiskers didn't wait a second longer. He simply ran for his life.

Now he was very frightened. He was also feeling cold and hungry. He wished that he was still in the warm safety of Susie's bedroom with the other toys. Just as he was thinking that the outside world was perhaps a bit *too* exciting, he heard the sound of a truck approaching. It suddenly stopped, its glaring headlights shining straight at him. On the side of the truck were the words STRAY CAT CATCHER.

Out of the truck stepped a man carrying a big net.
Catswhiskers thought he knew just who that net was for, and
decided that it was definitely time to go!

Without thinking about the dangers he might find himself in
if he came face to face again with gangs of sharp-clawed cats or
fierce, barking dogs, he ran back towards Susie's house as fast as
his velvet legs could carry him. At last he reached the window
and jumped thankfully back inside.

Snuggled down again on the warm bed with all his familiar
friends around him, Catswhiskers decided that perhaps this was
the best life for a pajama case cat after all.

TEA WITH THE QUEEN

Teddy bear, teddy bear,
Where have you been?
I've been up to London to visit the queen!

I went to her palace,
And knocked at the gate,
And one of her soldiers said, please would I wait?

Then one of her footmen,
All dressed in red,
Led me inside, saying, step this way, Ted!

And there in a huge room,
High on her throne,
Sat the poor queen, taking tea all alone.

She said, how delightful,
Sit down, fill your tum!
And soon we were chattering just like old chums!

And when time came to leave,
She shook hands and then,
She said, come back soon, we must do it again!

TEN LITTLE TEDDIES

Ten little teddies, standing in a line,
One of them went fishing, so then there were nine.

Nine little teddies, marching through a gate,
One stopped to tie his shoe, so then there were eight.

Eight little teddies, floating up in heaven,
One fell down and broke his crown,
so then there were seven.

Seven little teddies, doing magic tricks,
One made himself disappear, so then there were six.

Six little teddies, about to take a dive,
One of them was scared of heights, so then there were five.

Five little teddies, running on the shore,
One went surfing in the waves, so then there were four.

Four little teddies, eating cakes for tea,
One of them was feeling sick, so then there were three.

Three little teddies, heading for the zoo,
One of them hopped on a bus, so then there were two.

Two little teddies, playing in the sun,
One of them got sunburnt, so then there was one.

One little teddy, who's had lots of fun,
It's time for him to go to sleep, so now there are none.

LEAP FROG

"Whee! Look at me! Look at me!" yelled Springy, the frog, as he went leaping through the air, jumping from one lily pad to the other with a great splash. "I'm the bounciest frog in the whole wide world! Whee!"

"Tut, tut!" quacked Mother Duck. "That young frog is a nuisance. He never looks where he's going, and he doesn't mind who he splashes."

"Quite dreadful," agreed Downy, the swan. "And he makes so much noise. Sometimes it's hard to hear yourself think!"

But Springy wasn't listening. He was far too busy jumping across the lily pads as high as he could.

"Come on!" he called to the little ducklings. "Come over here, we'll have a diving contest!"

The ducklings shook their tails with excitement as they hurried across the pond towards him, then splashed about ducking and diving.

"He's a bad influence on our youngsters," Mother Duck went on. "If only something could be done about him."

"I suppose it's just high spirits," said Downy. "He'll grow out of it."

But Springy didn't grow out of it — he grew worse. He would wake everyone up at the crack of dawn, singing loudly at the top of his croaky voice:

"Here comes the day, it's time to play, hip hooray, hip hooray!" And he would leap from place to place, waking up the ducks and swans in their nests, calling down Rabbit's burrow, and shouting into Water Rat's hole in the bank. Of course, Springy just thought that he was being friendly. He didn't realize that everyone was getting fed up with him.

"I'm all for a bit of fun," said Water Rat. "But young Springy always takes things too far."

Then one day, Springy appeared almost bursting with excitement.

"Listen everyone," he called. "There's going to be a jumping competition on the other side of the pond. All the other frogs from miles around are coming. But I'm sure to win, because I'm the bounciest frog in the whole wide world!" And with that he jumped high up in the air, just to prove it was true.

The day of the contest dawned, and everyone gathered at the far side of the pond to watch the competition. Springy had never seen so many frogs in one place before.

"Wait till they see how high I can jump!" he said, leaping up and down in excitement.

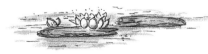

But to Springy's amazement, all the frogs could jump high, and far too. They sprang gracefully across the lily pads, cheered on by the crowd.

Springy was going to have to jump higher and further than ever if he wanted to win. At last it was his turn. "Good luck!" cried the ducklings.

Springy took his place on the starting pad, then gathering all his strength, he leapt up high and flew through the air, further and further, past the finish line, and on, until – GULP! He landed right in crafty Pike's waiting open mouth! As usual, Springy had not been looking where he was going!

The naughty pike swallowed Springy in one gulp, then dove down and hid in the middle of the pond. Everyone looked around in dismay – there was nothing they could do. Springy was gone.

Well, there was no doubt about it. Springy had jumped the highest, and the furthest.

"I declare Springy the winner," Warty, the toad, who had organised the contest, said glumly. So everyone went home, feeling sad and empty.

After that, things were much quieter for the other folk that lived around the pond.

But instead of enjoying the peace, they found that they rather missed Springy.

"He was a cheery little frog," said Downy.

"My young ones miss him terribly," said Mother Duck. "I suppose he did keep them busy."

But deep in the pond, Pike was feeling sorry for himself. He thought he'd been very clever catching that frog, but he'd had terrible indigestion ever since. You see, Springy was still busy jumping away inside him! Pike rose up to the top of the water, and gulped at the air. And as he did so, out jumped Springy!

Everyone was delighted to see him, and cheered as they gave him the medal for winning the jumping contest.

"This is wonderful," said Springy. "But I have learned my lesson — from now on I'll look before I leap!" and he hopped away quietly to play with the ducklings.

33

WOBBLY BEAR

Mr and Mrs Puppety owned an old-fashioned toy shop. They made toys by hand in a room at the back of the shop. But they were getting old and their eyesight was bad.

"It's time we got an apprentice toymaker," said Mr Puppety to his wife. They soon found a young lad called Tom to work for them. He worked hard and carefully. He spent his first week making a teddy bear. When he had finished he showed the bear to Mr and Mrs Puppety.

"He looks very cuddly," said Mrs Puppety.

Tom was pleased that they liked his bear and he went off home whistling happily.

"He is a lovely bear," said Mr Puppety, "but his head is a bit wobbly."

"I know," said his wife, "but it's Tom's first try. Let's just put him up there on the shelf with the other teddy bears."

That night Wobbly Bear sat on the shelf and started to cry. He had heard what Mr and Mrs Puppety had said about him.

"What's wrong?" asked Brown Bear, who was sitting next to him.

"My head is on wobbly," sobbed Wobbly Bear.

"Does it hurt?" asked Brown Bear.

"No," replied Wobbly Bear.

"Then why are you crying?" asked Brown Bear.

"Because nobody will want to buy a wobbly bear. I'll be left in this shop forever and nobody will ever take me home and love me," he cried.

"Don't worry," said Brown Bear. "We've all got our faults, and you look fine to me. Just try your best to look cute and cuddly and you'll soon have someone to love you." This made Wobbly Bear feel much happier and he soon fell fast asleep.

The next day the shop was full of people, but nobody paid any attention to Wobbly Bear. Then a little boy looked up at the shelf and cried, "Oh, what a lovely bear. Can I have that one, Daddy?"

Wobbly Bear's heart lifted as the little boy's daddy reached up to his shelf. But he picked up Brown Bear instead and handed him to the little boy. Wobbly Bear felt sadder than ever. Nobody wanted him. All of his new friends would get sold and leave the shop, but he would be left on the shelf gathering dust. Poor old Wobbly Bear!

Now, Mr and Mrs Puppety had a little grand-daughter called Jessie who loved to visit the shop and play with the toys. All the toys loved her because she was gentle and kind. It so happened that the next time she came to visit it was her birthday, and her grandparents told her she could choose any toy she wanted as her present.

"I know she won't choose me," thought Wobbly Bear sadly. "Not with all these other beautiful toys to choose from."

39

But to Wobbly's amazement, Jessie looked up and pointed at his shelf and said, "I'd like that wobbly bear please. No one else will have a bear quite like him."

Mr Puppety smiled and gave Wobbly to Jessie. She hugged and kissed him, and Wobbly felt so happy he almost cried. She took him home and put a smart red bow around his neck ready for her birthday party. He felt very proud indeed.

Soon the other children arrived, each carrying their teddy bears under their arms.

Wobbly Bear could not believe his eyes when he saw the little boy with his friend Brown Bear!

"I'm having a teddy bears' picnic," Jessie explained to him, hugging him tight. All of the children and the bears had a wonderful time, especially Wobbly. He had found a lovely home, met his old friend and made lots of new ones.

"See, I told you not to worry," said Brown Bear.

"I know," said Wobbly. "And I never will again."

The Three Little Pigs

Once upon a time there were three little pigs who lived on a farm with their mother and father. They decided that, although they were just little pigs, they were quite grown up enough to make their way in the big wide world, so one day they set off together to make their fortunes.

After they had walked for quite some time, one of the little pigs started to feel tired. Just then, a farmer went by on his hay cart.

"Hey, stop cart," the first little pig yelled. "You stronger brothers go on without me," he said. "This hay is light enough and soft enough for my house." And with that his brothers left the little pig with his pile of hay, and carried on their journey.

A little further down the road, the second little pig grew very
tired. Just then, they passed by a forester cutting wood.

"Would you sell me some of your wood?" asked the second little
pig. "This wood isn't too heavy and it isn't too rough for my house
– it's just right." And with that the third little pig carried on his
journey. Soon, even the third little pig grew very tired, and up
ahead he spotted a builder making a wall out of stone.

"Aha," he thought, "that's exactly what I need to build my
house, as it's strong and tough, just like me." And so he bought
some stone and built himself a house.

That evening, just as the first little pig was settling comfortably in his bed of hay, he heard a rustling outside the house. He easily parted the hay with his hands to look outside, and gulped in fright when he saw the big bad wolf looking at him greedily.

"Little piggy, little piggy, will you let me in?"

"Not on the hairs of my chinny chin chin, I will not let you in," shuddered the first little pig.

"Then I'll huff, and I'll puff, and I'll blow your house down," said the big bad wolf.

And sure enough, he gave a little huff, and he gave a little puff, and with very little effort he blew the house down. Before the straw had settled to the ground, the little pig ran away as fast as his little legs would carry him to the home of his nearest brother.

The next evening, just as the two brothers were sitting down
at their wooden table to eat their dinner, they heard scratching
and sniffing outside the house. They peeked through the wooden
window and gasped in alarm when they saw the big bad wolf
staring at them hungrily. His stomach rumbled loudly.

"Little piggies, little piggies, will you let me in?"

"Not on the hairs of our chinny chin chins,
we will not let you in," trembled the little pigs.

"Then I'll huff, and I'll puff, and
I'll blow your house down,"
said the big bad wolf.

And sure enough, he huffed a bit, and he puffed a bit, and with a bit of effort he blew the house down. Before the planks of wood had crashed to the ground, the two pigs ran away as fast as their little legs would carry them to the home of their brother.

The next evening, just as the three brothers were making the fire to warm their toes, they heard crunching and crashing outside the house. The third little pig pulled a tiny stone out of the wall to make a peephole, and they all shrieked in terror when they saw the big bad wolf staring at them ravenously. His stomach grumbled even louder, and he was smacking his lips with glee at the feast waiting just a short breath away!

"Little piggies, little piggies, will you let me in?"

"Not on the hairs of our chinny chin chins, we will not let you in," quaked the three little pigs.

"Then I'll huff, and I'll puff, and I'll blow your house down," said the big bad wolf.

And sure enough, he took a big huff, and he took a big puff, and with a big effort he blew. But the house didn't blow down. So he took a bigger huff, and he took a bigger puff, and with the biggest of efforts he blew. But the house still didn't blow down. So he filled his lungs as full as he could and with a mighty effort he blew and blew and blew! And the house stayed up!

With that the big bad wolf started to climb up the stone wall to the chimney on the roof. The three little pigs looked around the stark stone room and then at each other in dismay – there was nowhere in here to hide, and nowhere left to run. They would have to stand and fight the big bad wolf!

Suddenly one of the little pigs had an idea, and whispered it into the ears of his brothers. They all ran over to the fireplace and hooked a huge pot of water over the roaring fire. They heard the wolf climb into the chimney. The water in the pot started to steam. They heard the wolf climbing down the chimney. The water started to bubble. They heard the wolf slide the rest of the way down the chimney and he landed splash in the middle of the pot of now boiling water. PLOP!

"AAARRRRHHHHH!" screamed the big bad wolf, leaping immediately out of the boiling pot. The three little pigs ran around the room trying to get away from the wolf, as the big bad wolf ran around the room trying to cool down, until eventually he ran straight through the stone wall, leaving a huge big bad wolf-shaped hole, and carried on running and screaming and shouting all the way through the woods. That was the last they ever saw of the big bad wolf.

The three little pigs knew they had beaten the wolf, and he would never trouble them again, so they decided to build a brand new, comfortable house to live in. They built the walls of tough, strong stone. They made tables of smooth, warm wood, and they gathered lots of sweet-smelling, soft fresh hay to make comfortable beds. It was the best house in the world, and they all lived in it happily ever after.

HAPPY HIPPOPOTAMUS

Hey! look at me,
A happy hippopotamus,
Covered with mud
From my head to my bottom-us!
Squishing and squelching
And making an awful fuss,
Rolling around in my bath!

I like to blow bubbles
Breath out through my nose-es,
To wriggle and jiggle
The mud through my toes-es,
And would you believe it
That I smell like roses,
When I come out of my bath!

To the tune of 'Oh, dear, what can the matter be?'

Esmerelda the Ragdoll

At the back of the toy cupboard on a dark and dusty shelf lay Esmerelda the rag doll. She lay on her back and stared at the shelf above, as she had done for a very long time. It seemed to Esmerelda that it was many years since she had been lifted up by Clara, her owner, and even longer since she had been out in the playroom with the other toys. Now her lovely yellow hair was all tangled and her beautiful blue dress was creased, torn and faded. Each time Clara opened the toy cupboard door, Esmerelda hoped very much that she would be chosen, but Clara always played with the newer toys at the front of the cupboard. Every time Clara put her toys back in the cupboard, Esmerelda felt herself being pushed further towards the back. It was very uncomfortable and indeed, Esmerelda might have suffocated if it wasn't for a hole at the back of the cupboard, which enabled her to breathe.

These days Esmerelda felt very lonely. Until recently a one-eyed teddy bear had been beside her on the shelf. Then one day he had fallen through the hole at the back of the cupboard and was never seen again. Esmerelda missed him dreadfully, for he had been a lovely old teddy with a gentle nature. Now she, too, could feel herself being pushed towards the hole. She felt a mixture of excitement and fright at the prospect of falling through it. Sometimes she imagined that she would land on a soft feather bed belonging to a little girl who would really love her. At other times she thought that the hole led to a terrifying land full of monsters.

One day Esmerelda heard Clara's mother say, "Now Clara, today you must tidy up the toy cupboard and clear out all those old toys you no longer play with."

Esmerelda could see Clara's small hands reaching into the cupboard. She couldn't bear the thought of being picked up by the little girl and then discarded. "There's only one thing to do," she said to herself. She wriggled towards the hole, closed her eyes and jumped. Esmerelda felt herself falling, and then she landed with a bump on something soft.

"Watch out, my dear!" said a familiar voice from underneath her. Esmerelda opened her eyes and saw that she had landed on One-eyed Ted.

The two toys were so overjoyed to see each other again that they hugged one another. "What shall we do now?" cried Esmerelda.

"I have an idea," said Ted. "There's a rusty old toy car over there. I wanted to escape in it, but I can't drive with only one eye. What do you think? Shall we give it a go?"

"Yes, yes!" exclaimed Esmerelda, climbing into the driver's seat.

By now One-eyed Ted had found the key and was winding up the car. "Away we go!" he called as they sped off.

"Where are we going?" shouted Esmerelda.

"To the beach," replied Ted.

"Which way is it?" asked Esmerelda, holding on to her yellow hair streaming behind her in the wind.

"I don't know. We'll have to ask the way," said Ted.

Rounding a bend, they came across a black cat crossing the road. "Excuse me," called Ted, "could you tell us the way to the beach?"

Now, as you know, cats hate water. "Whatever do they want to go near water for? Why should I help them?" thought the cat. "It's the other side of that mountain," he growled as he ran off.

On sped the rusty car, and up the mountainside. When they reached the top of the mountain they met a sheep. Now, as you know, sheep never listen properly. "Excuse me," said Esmerelda, "where can we find the beach?"

Well, the silly sheep thought Esmerelda was asking where they could find a peach! "Down there," she bleated, nodding towards an orchard in the valley below.

Esmerelda and Ted leaped back into the car and sped off down the mountainside, but when they reached the orchard there was no sign of water, of course – just a lot of peach trees.

Once again they scratched their heads in puzzlement. Just then a mole popped his head out of the earth. "Excuse me," said Ted, "would you happen to know how we can find the sea?"

Now the mole was very wise, but unfortunately he was also, as you know, very short sighted. He peered at Esmerelda's blue dress. "That patch of blue must surely be a river, and rivers run into the sea," he thought.

"Just follow that river," he said, "and you'll end up at the sea. Good day!" And with that he disappeared under ground again.

Esmerelda and Ted looked even more puzzled, for there was no sign of a river in the orchard. "Oh well," sighed Esmerelda, "perhaps we'll never find the beach."

"Don't give up," said Ted. "We'll surely find it in the end." They climbed back in the rusty car and set off again. After a short while the car started to splutter and then it came to a complete halt at the side of the road. "What shall we do now?" cried Esmerelda.

"We'll just have to wait here and see what happens," said Ted. It seemed like a very long time that they sat beside the road. At long last they heard footsteps, and then Esmerelda felt herself being picked up.

"Look – it's a dear old tatty rag doll," said a voice. Esmerelda looked up and saw that she was being carried by a little girl.

Ted and the rusty car had been picked up by the girl's father. "We'll take them home and look after them," the man said.

Now they were in a real car and before long the toys found themselves in a house. The little girl carried Esmerelda, One-eyed Ted and the rusty car upstairs to her bedroom and put them down on a window sill. "I'll be back soon," she whispered.

Esmerelda looked out of the window and nearly danced for joy. "Look, look Ted," she shouted. For out of the window she could see the road, and beyond the road was a beach and then the sea. "We reached the beach after all," she cried.

Esmerelda, Ted and the rusty car lived happily in the house beside the sea. Esmerelda's hair was brushed and plaited and she was given a beautiful new dress. Ted had a new eye sewn on and could see properly again. The rusty car was painted and oiled. Most days the little girl took her new toys down to the beach to play with, and the days in the dark toy cupboard were soon forgotten. The little girl used to tell her friends the story of how she had found her three best toys lying beside the road one day. And as for the toys, well, they sometimes talked about that strange day when they had such an adventure – and they'd burst out laughing.

LITTLE DOG LOST

"Brrr," shivered Scruffy. "It's cold tonight."

"Well, snuggle up closer to me," said his mom.

"It's not fair," Scruffy grumbled. "Why do we have to sleep outside in the cold? The cats are allowed to sleep inside, in nice warm baskets!"

"We're farm dogs, dear," said Mom. "We have to be tough, and work hard to earn our keep."

"I'd rather be a cat," mumbled Scruffy. "All they do is wash themselves, eat and sleep."

"We don't have such a bad life," said Mom. "Now stop feeling sorry for yourself, and get some rest. We've got a lot of work to do tomorrow."

The next day, Scruffy woke early and trotted down the lane for a walk. He ran through the grass, chasing rabbits, and sniffing at the flowers.

Now, usually when he got to the end of the lane he stopped and turned back. But today, he saw a big red truck parked outside a house there. The back of the truck was open, and Scruffy thought he would just climb inside and take a look.

The truck was full of furniture. At the back was a big armchair with soft cushions. Scruffy clambered onto it. "I could doze all day, like a cat!" he told himself. He closed his eyes and before he knew it he had fallen fast asleep.

Scruffy awoke some time later with a sharp jolt.

"Oh, no, I fell asleep!" he groaned. "I'd better hurry back. We've got a busy day ahead!"

But then he saw that the truck doors were closed! He could hear voices outside.

"Oh, dear, I'll be in trouble if I get found in here," thought Scruffy, and he hid behind the chair.

The back of the truck opened and Scruffy peered out. Two men started unloading the furniture.

When Scruffy was sure that no one was looking, he crept out of the truck, but he was no longer in the countryside where he lived! He was in a big noisy town, full of buildings and cars.

Poor Scruffy had no idea where he was!

"The truck must have carried me away," thought Scruffy, feeling frightened.

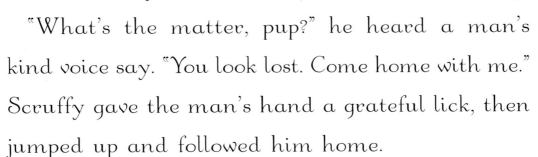

All day long, Scruffy roamed around trying to find his way home, feeling cold, tired and hungry. At last, he lay down and began to howl miserably.

"What's the matter, pup?" he heard a man's kind voice say. "You look lost. Come home with me." Scruffy gave the man's hand a grateful lick, then jumped up and followed him home.

When they arrived at the man's house Scruffy sat on the doorstep, hoping the man might bring him some food out to eat. But the man said, "Come on in, you can't stay out there."

Scruffy followed the man in, and found a little poodle waiting to meet him. Scruffy stared at her in amazement. What had happened to her fur?

"You'd better take a bath before supper," said the man, looking at Scruffy's dirty white coat. The man washed him in a big tub, then brushed his tangled coat. Scruffy howled miserably. What had he done to deserve such punishment?

"Don't you like it?" asked the poodle, shyly.

"No, I don't," said Scruffy. "All this washing and cleaning is for cats!"

Next the man gave them supper — small bowls of dry pellets. Scruffy sniffed at them in disgust. He was used to chunks of meat and a nice big bone.

"This looks like cat food," said Scruffy, miserably.

After supper the poodle climbed into a big basket in the kitchen.

"I thought that belonged to a cat," said Scruffy. He tried sleeping in the basket but he was hot and uncomfortable. He missed counting the stars to help him fall asleep, and most of all he missed his mom.

"I want to go home," he cried, and big tears slipped down his nose.

The next day, the man put Scruffy on a lead and took him into town. He hated being dragged along, without being able to sniff at things.

Then, as they crossed the market place, Scruffy heard a familiar bark, and saw his mom's head hanging through the window of the farmer's truck! He started to howl, dragged the man over to where the truck was parked, then leapt up at the window barking excitedly. The farmer could hardly believe it was Scruffy — he had never seen him so clean! The man explained how he had found Scruffy, and the farmer thanked the man for taking such good care of him.

On the way back home, Scruffy told his mom all about his adventure and what had happened.

"I thought you had run away because you didn't like being a farm dog," she said gently.

"Oh, no, Mom," said Scruffy, quickly. "I love being a farm dog. I can't wait to get home to a nice big juicy bone and our little bed beneath the stars!"

HIGH JUMP

The Shrew said to the Kangaroo,
"I can jump as high as you!"
Laughed Kanga, "How can that be true
Of one so small, please tell me, do!"

Said Shrew, "I'll show you, then you'll see,
I'll jump so high, I'll reach that tree!
But first of all you must agree,
To show your jumping skills to me!"

Then Kanga bounced into the air,
So busy he was unaware
That Shrew was clinging to his hair
To reach the treetop – most unfair!

Back Kanga landed on the ground,
"Your turn," he said, and spun around.
"Up here!" called Shrew, a distant sound.
"Well," said Kanga, "I'll be bound!"

GREEDY BEAR

If there is one thing in the whole wide world that a teddy bear likes more than anything it is buns — big sticky cinnamon buns with sugary tops, and squishy middles. A teddy bear will do almost anything for a bun. But for one greedy little teddy bear called Clarence, sticky buns were to be his unsticking!

Rag Doll baked the most wonderful buns in the little toy cooker. She baked big buns and small buns, iced buns and cinnamon buns, raisins buns and poppy-seeds buns, and even hot-cross buns! She shared them out amongst the toys in the playroom, and everybody loved them. But no-one loved them as much as Clarence.

"If you will give me your bun, I'll polish your boots!" he'd say to Tin Soldier.

And sometimes if Tin Soldier was not feeling too hungry, he'd agree. There was always someone who would give Clarence their bun in return for a favor, and sometimes Clarence would eat five or six buns in one day!

Then he'd be busy washing the dolls' dresses, brushing Scotty Dog's fur, or cleaning the toy policeman's car. He would even stand still and let the clown throw custard pies at him!

69

So you see, Clarence was not a lazy bear, but he was a greedy bear, and in spite of all his busy-ness, he was becoming a rather plump little greedy bear. All those buns were starting to show around his middle, and his fur was beginning to strain at the seams!

Then one day Clarence rushed into the playroom full of excitement. His owner, Penny, had told him that next week she was taking him on a teddy bears' picnic.

"She says there will be honey sandwiches and

ice-cream and cookies — and lots and lots of buns!"
Clarence told the others, rubbing his hands
together. "I can hardly wait! In fact all this
excitement has made me hungry, so I think I'll
have a bun." And he took a big sticky bun out
from under a cushion where he'd hidden it earlier.

"Oh, Clarence!" said Rabbit. "One of these days
you will simply go pop!"

"Just be happy I don't like carrots!" said
Clarence with a smile.

Well, that week Clarence was busier than ever. Every time he thought about the picnic it made him feel hungry, and then he'd have to find someone who'd let him have their bun. He ate bun after bun, and would not listen when Rag Doll warned him that his back seam was starting to come undone.

The day of the teddy bears' picnic dawned, and Clarence yawned and stretched, smiling to himself with excitement. But as he stretched he felt a strange popping sensation all down his stomach. He tried to sit up in bed, but to his alarm he found he could not move. He looked down to see that the seams around his tummy had popped open, and his stuffing was spilling out all over the bed!

"Help!" he cried. "I'm exploding!"

Just then, Penny woke up. "Oh, Clarence!" she cried when she saw him. "I can't take you to the teddy bears' picnic like that!"

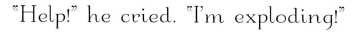

Penny showed Clarence to her mommy, who said he would have to go to the toy hospital.

Clarence was away from the playroom for a whole week, but when he came back he was as good as new. Some of his stuffing had been taken out, and he was all sewn up again.

He had had lots of time to think in the hospital about what a silly greedy bear he had been. How he wished he had not missed the picnic. The other teddies said it was the best day out they had ever had. Penny had taken Rabbit instead.

"It was terrible," moaned Rabbit. "Not a carrot in sight. I did save you a bun though." And he pulled a big sticky bun out of his pocket.

"No thank you, Rabbit," said Clarence. "Funnily enough, I've gone off buns!"

Of course, Clarence did not stop eating buns for long, but from then on he stuck to one a day. And he still did favors for the others, only now he did them for free!

One, Two, Three, Four, Five

One, two, three, four, five,

Once I caught a fish alive.

Six, seven, eight, nine, ten,

Then I let him go again.

Why did you let him go?

Because he bit my finger so!

Which finger did he bite?

This little finger on the right.

The Lion
and the Unicorn

The Lion and the Unicorn
Were fighting for the crown;
The Lion beat the Unicorn
All around the town.
Some gave them white bread,
And some gave them brown;
Some gave them plum cake,
And drummed them out of town.

There Was a Crooked Man

There was a crooked man
And he walked a crooked mile,
He found a crooked sixpence
Against a crooked stile.
He brought a crooked cat
Which caught a crooked mouse
And they all lived together
In a little crooked house.